## Praise for Andrés Neuman

"Good readers will find something that can be found only in great literature, the kind written by real poets, a literature that dares to venture into the dark with open eyes and that keeps its eyes open no matter what."
—Roberto Bolaño, *Between Parentheses*

"It is impossible to classify Andrés Neuman: each of his books is a new language adventure, guided by the intelligence and the pleasure of words. He never ceases to surprise us and is, doubtlessly, one of the most daring writers in Latin American literature, willing to change, challenge and explore, always with a unique elegance."
—Mariana Enriquez, author of *Things We Lost in the Fire*

"*Traveler of the Century* doesn't merely respect the reader's intelligence: it sets out to worship it.... A beautiful, accomplished novel: as ambitious as it is generous, as moving as it is smart."
—Juan Gabriel Vásquez, author of *The Sound of Things Falling*

"*Talking to Ourselves* is both brilliant and wise, and Andrés Neuman is destined to be one of the essential writers of our time."
—Teju Cole, author of *Open City*

"This is writing of a quality rarely encountered … When you read Neuman's beautiful novel, you realize a very high bar has been set."
—*The Guardian*

"A work of true beauty and scintillating intelligence by a writer of prodigious talents … Books as stimulating, erudite and humane as this do not come along very often."
—*The Independent*

ALSO BY ANDRÉS NEUMAN
IN ENGLISH TRANSLATION

*Traveler of the Century*
*Talking to Ourselves*
*The Things We Don't Do*
*How To Travel Without Seeing*
*Fracture*
*Bariloche*
*Love Training*
*Once Upon Argentina*
*Sensitive Anatomy*

# A FATHER IS BORN
## by Andrés Neuman

Translated from the Spanish by Robin Myers

Originally published as *Umbilical* (2022) and *Pequeño hablante* (2024) by Alfaguara
Copyright © Andrés Neuman, 2022, 2024
Translation copyright © Robin Myers, 2025

First Open Letter edition, 2025
All rights reserved

Library of Congress Catalog-in-Publication Data: TK.
ISBN (pb): 978-1-960385-41-3 | ISBN (ebook): 978-1-960385-42-0

Cover design by Alban Fischer

Printed on acid-free paper.

Open Letter Books
University of Rochester, Morey Hall 303, Rochester, NY 14627
www.openletterbooks.org

# A FATHER IS BORN
## by Andrés Neuman

# CONTENTS

I - Umbilical

The Imagination

The Apparition

And a Minimal Monologue


II - Small Speaker

1–95

A–Z

# I

~

# UMBILICAL

For my son Telmo, who gave me birth.
For Erika, artisan of light.

*Tell the man to give up tumult for the while*
*to wonder at the sight of baby's beauty.*
Anne Waldman

# THE IMAGINATION

# 1

I don't dare invoke you too early, lest you disappear. But what if superstition works the other way around, and naming you confirms that you're real?

You dangle by a thread. And yet you're not fragile, because you don't yet recognize your own fragility: you're more like ours.

Little by little, I'm birthed as I speak to you.

## 2

They look like a hippocampus, a space traveler, or some impossible fusion of the two. They float, unaware of us watching their primordial yoga.

Now she has two hearts. One is rebellious and entirely hers; the other, tiny, ours.

# 3

In the cave sketches of ultrasounds, we search for signs of the future.

"I think that's a hand."

"The brain's lighting up."

In the beginning were the genes awaiting their rhythm, their penmanship, all the revolutions we won't know how to read.

# 4

Hiding their sex onscreen, they improvise a modesty yet unknown to them. Smudged at the center, they shirk labels, mischievous.

"Do you want to know?"

"No."

"Yes."

"We're not sure."

May you turn out to be a girl, a boy, both, neither. May you pay no mind to the genital scribble, its semantic blueprint.

And rewrite it with and over time, and feel its tingle, and celebrate it.

# 5

Maybe the strange authority of choosing a name is something like the act of inaugurating a new language with its first word. Just as fertile, just as artificial. Mario? Julio? Marcelo? We utter you this way.

You deserve to be called whatever you want, once syllabic language dampens your mouth. But your mother and I will impose a name on you: that's our freedom and our act of violence.

At first you'll be who we say you are, and you'll learn to object with every babble.

# 6

They move in space, create space by moving. They're something of an electron and a pioneer swimmer. Do they sense limits as those same limits expand? Do they feel that they're floating of their own accord, or that reality oscillates?

It hammers at the walls, their grain of rice.

# 7

"More than their creator, I feel like their host," your mother confesses.

Now I imagine us in concentric circles: you travel within a reality within our reality, which exists within ceaseless curves. What am I, then, in this home where your mother's womb rocks and sways? Who do I inhabit?

I walk differently around this house. Its nooks and crannies receive me ahead of time, folding me as I search for the warmth you bring.

# 8

And I weep in the kitchen at how welcome you are. Not for lack of doubts (which I had) or fear (which I have), but because you've rowed right over them and into this place that smells of vegetables and fermented milk.

I spent my first year of life spitting up fluids, reality, sheer country. That's what I was told. How did I ever grow up among lacunae? I don't remember if I was welcomed there.

# 9

I didn't manage to cry when I was born. They say I just looked around a lot. And looking was toxic. There was dictatorship in the oxygen, exile and torture in our family. But—most of all—there was silence. A silence in its infancy.

And I came up in a school of virile nonsense where crying was elliptical, over-acting the opposite. And I saved my vaguely Jewish skin by escaping from what I needed most.

I was birthed once. I had no idea.

I was so afraid you'd come, my son, and find me. I hope I'll learn to cry as I should have.

## 10

Of course, we haven't summoned you into the pleasantest of times. There's a pandemic, quarantine, earthquakes challenging the foundations of the story. Your mother's land is a seismic one. This will mark your course.

Meanwhile, I wonder what accompanies you in your capsule. Minuscule tornados, placental storms, gusts of iron and vitamins? Do they rise, the tides of amniotic seas?

You arrive against the current. You're born surviving.

# 11

Your mother perceives you as a strain, a felicitous gas. That's what she tells me. The humble precision of her malaises reveals more of you to me than the obstetrics I'm so eager to study. It's by your symptoms, my son, that I come to recognize you in the body of love.

"He just poked me."

I don't know how it feels to feel you beyond the story: like a good character, you create reality while occupying time. What time is it in your world? It was late in mine, but dawn comes on little feet.

## 12

My voice, seeding, left you an echo. I sing into her belly. Are you there? Am I? Are we?

I sing to you all day long, not because I'm sure you can hear me, but so your ears will become real. Your mother is both conductor and instrument of this music that suffuses the skin, delving into her ripples. As you can see, she's quite a virtuoso.

"No, no, no. The head's over here."

I broadcast melodies without knowing if they'll reach you, if your uterine station will intercept me. Maybe you're singing too, and we just can't hear you. A note in the water, a fish in the stave.

# 13

Pregnant with questions, awareness dawns.

Can you hear the song of the future present? What does it sound like where you are, this language, its arbitrary beauty? Is there something umbilical about the vocal cords that speak your name? Does the placenta serve as a tuning fork? Do the genes meet the pitch if they resound? Is recognizing voices the same as love?

## 14

You can't yet open your eyelids. It'll take you a lifetime to debut the eyes behind them.

You can't yet open them, but you have kidneys, a liver, a brain, a minuscule sampling of fingernails. In whatever we call existence, translucency can be a barrier.

You can't yet open your eyes, and you're already teaching us to see.

# 15

"He's tense."

"He's intent."

I can tell you're my son in how intensely you move through the idea of mother. Music affects you, you're gifted at all-nighters, and you halt, bashful, in the sonogram's invented light.

Who knows who you'll turn into. I can't get a good look at your face, but I suspect we resemble each other.

# 16

The skin of the beloved belly is a windowpane that trembles between my fingers and yours. I sketch a fleeting message before you can even imagine what writing is.

"Read this. Tell me."

You reach out a hand, close and improbable as a stranger.

Pleased to meet you, son of mine. To be beginning what we'll both become.

# 17

I call you and you knock, you knock and I call. A luminous tap-tap. A dialogue of accents.

    These sudden bulges, these intermittencies in your mother's swift belly, are the first rhythm in the song we seek.

# 18

I wish I could stroke the foot that skirts the border, treading inside. I want to touch your steps, but can't: we're practically neighbors.

There you are, here I am, across a trifling abyss. As men are taught to be together.

# 19

You have no shortage of prenatal luxuries.

You disrupt the rest of your hostess, you sleep if she works.

Your hands have coined a sign language to speak in the dark.

Speechless chatterbox, you get hiccups of haste.

And you even allow yourself to yawn: life already bores you, because you're living.

## 20

Your folded eyes can now receive shades of light, like a sheet of paper pressed to the windowpane. I peer out at the one gleaming across from my table, try to decipher the message.

This framed instant, this partial beam, a precarious sun feeling its way along the wall.

## 21

When you open your eyes, you see darkness. The gift of eyelashes is your brand-new achievement. Now your blinking arranges the mirage of sight.

But your world is a world, even if you're its sole resident. This other one, after all, struggles with perspective. We're a nosy crowd who open our eyes, as you'll find out, only when it suits us.

## 22

Out and about, she feels like she's guiding you, showing you the place, recognizing it on your behalf. Now she thinks in chords. She talks to herself with you.

"Good morning."

"Good morning."

"Good morning."

And waking each day, regaining her agility, she suspects her belly has waned. That motherhood gets written during the hours of light, then rubbed out with sleep.

# 23

When she sneezes, the motherland shudders. He lives at the epicenter. I wonder if he'll take it for an external phenomenon or one of his own.

"Bless you," I tell them both.

I'm not sure who answers.

# 24

We sleep in profile, her belly in the hollow of my back, to keep you between our bodies.

We try to shelter you in parentheses, little morsel of time, and I can feel your commotion traveling the rope of vertebrae that will soon lift you up. This is how the future gathers at my back.

# 25

Your mother slumbers. Nighttime cyclist, you keep the sleep machine in motion, and your feet pedal her unconscious.

As you follow the curve of the hours, I rest a hand on your revolutions and we invent a way to fall asleep while laughing. How cheeky of you to run the night without even being born.

# 26

When we do what we did to make you, when we're alone in your slight company, when we press against each other and become a synthesis, when I enter into your mother and, somehow, I access you too, both of us restored to the origin, companions in the inaugural porn, I can feel our overlapping fates, hands over hands over hands.

# 27

"They're socks for when he's here."

"They're for when he gets here. Socks."

Gifts for absent feet: a peculiar custom of our tribe. Retracing to where we too once came, shoeing our ellipses.

Some remote ancestor must have been very cold before birth. Tomorrow's footsteps patter close.

## 28

The clothes arrive before the body, a ruckus of diminutive sleeves. What kind of ghost gets dressed beforehand?

I miss you without even knowing you. I can't hold you yet, so I envelop you.

## 29

I arrange your garments, measure your absent form. You're not with me or within me, but when I touch the fabric that omits you, I recognize myself.

    I'm the one awaiting you without gestation, a man baffled to be born a man, who clothes your shape and carefully folds, one by one, his limitations.

# 30

We invoked you, not sure you'd come. And one day you took the hint.

With an air of perennial promise, of an invitee playing hard to get, here you are, imposing your not-yet.

And your empty crib that fills the room to the brim.

# 31

"So when does he come into the world?"

"He's already in the world," we insist.

I like that you don't come even though you're here, encircling me with your clock. Waiting isn't the same as imagining you; a horizon is so much more than an ending.

You already inhabit the place by disrupting it. To live is a parenthesis. Belly. Hunger for time.

# 32

We learn to love you while you don't come: that's the other gestation.

You're an imminence that seizes our house, the order of all the things that will soon shed their prior functions and silently bid them farewell.

That's exactly how you roam your maternal environment, announcing, still invisible, the sacred violence of all perspective.

## 33

She'd say you make her feel old, and she'd mesmerize you with the sound of your own name. From your first babbles onward, you'd have chatted with her raspy voice.

More than taking you on walks, she'd have made you sit at coffee shops and concert halls. You'd have found her steaming from the mouth, filled with more wine than night, roughing up her organs while telling tales of the soul.

You'd have met her humming calluses, the musical vampire's mark on the left side of her neck. She'd probably gifted you one of her violins.

Since I don't have a mother, you have no grandmother. You're leaving me re-orphaned, son, by love alone.

# 34

*Carpe ventrem.* Make good use of your exact address: being in someone is a rare privilege. Take advantage of the space and lack of space: those choreographies. Maximize the feast of the digestive sky before your mouth starts working. Savor this life before your life, and given the chance in your kingdom of urea, proteins, and rhythm, remember this hand that seeks you. *Carpe ventrem.*

# 35

Clothes for the absent presence, meticulous possessions, liturgic luggage, all into the taxi of chance. Everything is so thoroughly planned that I suspect no news will break: the most important things burst forth unannounced, because their roots are vulnerable.

We arrive, they receive us, we rehearse the truth for a while, then return confusedly identical.

What can you sense awaiting you at the border? How much must you already know about the world, if you refuse to come out?

# 36

The light through the blinds of the dreaded hospital. The chemicals in the veins. And a murmur of horses from the indifferent monitor. Their gallop is swifter than the time they pursue.

Your mother feigns sleep, imitates it to see if sleep will admit her. She has an air of Goya's medicated Maja, her feet swollen, cloaked in the robe of a queen from another realm.

In my blue sweater and eye mask, just in case, I observe you without seeing you, barefoot of certainties, practicing how I'll feel.

# 37

"Is it like they said?"

"It's worse."

I can read her pain on the cardiotocograph, like a score. Her contractions seek the cadence; they harm her, giving rhythm to our son.

With the basso continuo of life in death and the other way around, the heart and uterus continue their counterpoint, a fugue straining toward a greater convergence. *Partum cantata.* The first word. This silence.

# 38

When your mother was born, the city went into a seismic trance. There were no other earthquakes so strong until today, now that it's time for your little head.

Your head approaching this shore atremble, the shudders of the body that bids you farewell and welcomes you here, this earthly body opening, the cracks of light, the blood unstitching the limits of the ground.

# 39

They're cruel to her—as if she were a heifer with limited rights—in the name of a cause that looks a lot like the power to refuse explanations.

"Grab there."

"Push!"

"All right, big push."

"Harder now."

I let them do her wrong for a right I can't see. I collaborate with this ritual of helplessness, jostling, and intravenous rage. Barely consensual, everything has the implicit quality of serum.

I don't rebel and I'm the humiliation of the accomplice, a body choosing silence.

# 40

So it was by force, my son, not the natural promises. Science pushed you, and terror, and a patriarchal handbook: civilization.

You wore the scarf of time, remnants from the whim of living.

With a kidney and a half of hope, you screamed that language is about being born however we can manage.

# THE APPARITION

# 41

We met without introductions in the small hours of anesthesia. I'm not sure what I sang to you, but you listened.

They brought you out naked. That's how you stripped me bare.

# 42

I hold one of your hands as you sleep. Just one, and with the slightest touch I can muster, so the other can reach into your unconscious.

I heft this wrist of improbable scale. I wait for your lungs to lift you, as if the air's own womb could rock you. If I take a breath and blow, please don't disappear.

# 43

By sanitary orders, that door is the customs clearance of a foreign future. We can't move or receive visitors. We can't exit our own birth.

This room compresses us between rules that no one seems to have written. The staff drips in and out, masked and punctual. The food cools like sleep.

We're three clumsy bodies trying to bond, by drawing closer, to see if they stick.

# 44

How is it that you have everything already in its place, brand new but complete? Where was your exacting blueprint? What miniature craftwork assembled you?

I devote myself to trimming these infinitesimal fingernails; I can't grasp how they were formed. I file them down with immaterial patience, diminish them by wisps, by blinks.

As capable of clinging to what they love as they are of harming us or hurting you. Ready, then, for life.

# 45

I don't recognize our house, so I reread it: it morphs in the light of your apparitions. Tomorrow's echoes play in the corners. After half a life without hurry, the furniture speeds up.

I search the rooms, but I'm no longer here.

# 46

Sleepless, we hallucinate our days. It's a sentinel ontology. This amalgam of spit, hours, milk, cuddles, doubts, rage.

"Ow."

"Now."

"That?"

"No."

"This?"

We give each other instructions stripped of syntax, eat one-armed, see double or halfway, heads smoldering inside. We roam, pilgrims in our own house, searching for a path.

And deep in the desert, the dunes of meaning insinuate their shapes.

# 47

You need transparent arms that can carry you where there are no objects, distractions, or stimuli. You can't seem to vanquish your own vigilance, my tiny attention-warrior.

In the distance, the sphinxes of your other hemisphere await you. They'll define you more than your mother or father ever could.

Never fear sleep: it will be your home, the first and final.

## 48

"It's not there anymore."

"It's gone."

"Now his belly button belongs to him."

This offshoot that's just fallen away, with its tubercular air, kept you bound to a memory you'll never have. It's yours and not. What do we get to keep of each experience that peels away?

As night presses in against the window, you begin the interminable task of learning who you are. Don't go thinking that my furred, memorious navel has ever figured it out.

# 49

Gorilla of love, you clutch at the hairs that spring from my sterile chest—there you persist, as if mistakes could burgeon with miracles. You shake them hard, uproot them like weeds.

Unable to feed you in this jungle of affections, we reforest.

# 50

When you nurse, you shine, brimming with a light half-loaned. Your skin is burnished in the dark, and you're transformed into a milky star.

"I think he's bigger than he was fifteen minutes ago."

I wish I could drink your edges, eat from your shadowspill. You're feeding me as you grow, too.

# 51

Her breasts flake, grow infected, disintegrate into your thinking. There's pain in keeping you fed, an insomniac trance, a nightmare mirrored.

"I don't like my breasts, but I like what they give."

And in the course of this paradox, the flesh of her flesh evolves into pronoun, a person apart.

# 52

Your whole soul is a body: a monk of organs. Cathedral-like, you echo when you cry. Whatever hurts you or keeps you awake hails from parts unknown, the destination of my please. Your needs attain the height of mystery.

If I could know what harms you, I'd be more than a father.

# 53

Sometimes, when your wails rise to the ceiling, I can only resort to delirious dance. I seek out your tantrum's visual field and start flailing my limbs, begging for the treasure of a new attention.

"Look. Here. Please."

Luckily, you find my desperation hilarious. You're entertained when I dance for you, although I certainly don't know how. Is it the marvel of bipedalism? Or is my clumsiness a comfort?

# 54

Your merchant father sells his back for inches of laughter. I collect my wages in recognition of your pre-verbal gums, trying to dignify this ludicrous exhaustion. My labor force depends on your means of producing delight. I regret to inform you that love negotiates, too.

# 55

Whenever you laugh, the glass I'm secretly transporting shatters. The mechanism is simple. You look at me, you laugh, it breaks.

Now my joy needs yours as ivy seeks the complicity of a tree trunk. Ivy, glass. Shadow, light. A fragile growth.

I laugh because you laugh: you've birthed the humor of a nearly old man. In your breathing trembles mine.

# 56

You distrust the environment you inhabited before birth. Your tiny feet begin to resist the water, like frogs in the wrong haiku. No fleeting splash, no hint at celebration. Your business is to protest in your own element, this defensive flotation.

Your baths are somehow circular, like this garish plastic tub: its unstable promise, its slippery gifts alarm you. Until, slowly, you reach some kind of sensory tuning and pleasure is confirmed.

But by then it's time to dry you off.

# 57

I don't photograph you just so you'll remember, son, but so you'll remember me. This is the hidden picture. The B-side of our album.

Smile, don't move. This is who we were.

# 58

Now you like the bath: it baptizes you. When you emerge from the water, I wrap you in a towel as white as the first on earth, I hug you to my chest, you shut your eyes. I'm not sure if we're returning to the sacred moment of your birth or retreating together all the way back to mine, before we both existed.

In this trance of communion, I beg the instant not to pass, may you not grow up too fast, may I never grow old, may the end be nothing but a plot device, may I never know another love, no other love than this.

Then your nearly translucent back rests against the mattress, tears and laughter resume, and our life pretends to carry on.

# 59

Inner astronomer, you like to gaze up at the heights of our house. Your mission is always slightly higher than my shoulder. Your explorer-forehead, your mouth wider than light, the ideas circling in the constellation of your iris.

When I watch you watching, I learn about space and its relative scales. You don't pay attention, you create it. Fascination in pursuit of its object.

# 60

There's an art to this carefree way of pissing and shitting: it's taken generations of theorists repressing the urge, handling the bow that tenses the line between instinct and prejudice, turning philosophy entirely upside down, for you to fill my two hands with your declaration of here and now.

# 61

"Again?"

Your sphincter is an anthem, always singing. It makes you laugh with glee, with doing what can be done.

I'm the apprehensive sort who tries to celebrate each libertarian spurt. I've just taken the step between dodging you and baring myself, between shelter and the open air. And this small repulsion is devotion now.

Our house is full of excrement, bundled up like offerings. I separate and heft them with care, attending to their alchemy. This pungent gold, which transforms the environment that nurses you, has soiled my love and saved it.

# 62

Unless my clothes are new, or newly washed, you have no interest in vomiting onto them with your most winning smile. It's like the bottle smashed onto a ship when it sets sail. (Do those rituals still exist? You force me to doubt my own imagery.)

This drool, with clumps of mother, acidic and holy, warms the shoulder that soothes you.

# 63

"Ba."

"Da."

"Ta-*ta*."

"Ta-*teh*."

We play at exchanging sounds that have no prior meaning, just vowels hungry for semantics. You open your mouth as if to tell me what you don't say. Our lips draw closer. We yelp an a that's almost e. And we're two infatuated creatures with our entire language ahead of us.

"A-*eh*."

"You sure?"

"A-*eh*."

# 64

With shoddy aim, we roll a multicolored ball between us. It spins and clatters. It comes and goes from your hands to mine; we lose it in a corner. Then I get up and we try again until our next act of clumsiness.

This, more or less, is what communication with your fellows will be like. You could say we're practicing.

## 65

Both stone and feather, your whole head fits in the palm of my hand. But its pre-verbal notions feel so far away.

How much do you know about yourself, what do you guess about me? Direct interpreters, no matter how little heed you pay to pronouns, your senses understand.

# 66

In light pale as bone, in flat black and white, you swim through the dark. The screen frames you like a fiction.

I've become addicted to beholding you this way, in your slowest version: the occasional turn, a finger in your mouth, a casual sigh, a pout or two.

It's a post-natal sonogram. You're dreaming yesterday.

# 67

Standing in the kitchen, facing the screen, I study the fluctuations of your slumber.

Your tiny water-chest, your windmill-arms, your sapling-head, legs riding horseless. So small that your own toes don't yet fit on your feet.

# 68

What is this unmanageable doodad? What is it doing there, this bunch of prehensile appendages that remind you of who knows what? Who put these hands in your hands: so wholly yours, so wholly foreign?

Watching you, I seem to understand. The discoveries were always in plain sight. The greatest mysteries, within reach.

# 69

"Who's that baby?"

"Baby, who's that?"

You reply with your mouth and without words: facing an intruder as agile as yourself, you want to gulp him down. Your image dissolves in the steam.

Don't rush to absorb it. When you do recognize it, you'll feel even stranger.

# 70

Your mouth teems with an occurrence that you'll come to make more or less your own; something that skitters between mischief and a nervous tic. Smiling, like all labor, can wear you out.

"A-*eh*."

You're right: it's no small feat to have fun without help.

# 71

You're developing a moral nose. I sense your sneezes humming with response, even opprobrium. Snot, your tiny barricade. There's something in the air that isn't quite your business.

# 72

We spend the day in each other's arms, lulling ourselves to sleep in a mutual dependency. You pretend I take care of you, and we grow more and more into childhood, two ages drawing closer.

I'm on my way, I'll wait for you here.

# 73

We sprawl out to nibble at our fingers, shoulders, hours. The game is to taste each other; we evolve into a slurping species. We exchange ancestral drool. We speak a language of suction.

Your skin tastes of a lemon's debut with a subtext of milk, a sweetness predating the mouth's own school.

I wonder what my hairs taste like, my wrinkles, the memento of a wound.

# 74

You suck at what's real. That object acquires existence while documented by your mouth. My hand is only my hand if your gums sample their contours; I exist insofar as you taste me. Edible consciousness. Congratulations.

After studying it with gourmet attention, you select your left foot for your first bite. Is it salty? Does it taste of a step we'll take someday?

You gnaw your heel, then your fist: a complete cycle in your extremities. You're made of beginnings, my light at the end.

# 75

Your zeal can't fit between your lips. I want to kiss your metaphysical mouth, eat what you eat, gulp down your appetite.

I fear I've caught your cannibalistic anxiety. Frankly, I'm tempted to devour you. But don't worry, it's tradition.

# 76

We roll around on the floor, playing with things that play with us, tumbling on the rug and in time. We yell without the rules that will soon serve as our perimeter. Something will be lost in these developments; I long for them and they frighten me.

I don't want to rush: I'm guided by your present, you hedonistic passenger of the afternoon, my tiny untheoretical anarchist. Desire is just the law of starting over.

We roll around together and you'll never remember this moment, when you were so wise you knew nothing.

## 77

I admire how dauntless you are, you diapered avant-gardist. You surrender to the night's rage, to the stage of the street, to the makeshift party, free of all the doubts I find so paralyzing.

Unwitting radical, you specialize in the performance of being alive. Comfy in your episteme, which begins with the body.

# 78

Ever since you started suspecting the laws of cause and effect, your means of entertainment have changed: now you're delighted in advance, already celebrating what you hope will happen.

"Ha."

A laugh, so we joke.

"Huh?"

An answering shriek if you're alone, and we're off.

"Oh."

A look of surprise for the game to begin.

Once you've lost the gifts of babyhood, only fiction will allow you such feats.

# 79

"Should I read him the one about the fish?"

"How about the one about the trees. It's tastier."

You sniff, touch, and bite the books that rain into your hands. You move from one color to the next: fruits dangling from the boughs of synesthesia.

Why pass your eyes over the page when you can eat a story whole?

# 80

In the book you're eating, there's a shy crab and a hollow turtle and a penguin who travels in his father's belly. A red string pulls him out into the open air. You're obsessed with tugging on the baby penguin. You want to watch, incessantly, this synopsis of delivery and separation.

Umbilical, the cord gleams between your fingers. You've become your own midwife.

# 81

You sleep with your fox. Only he can lull you. If the furry, conspiratorial fox didn't exist, no fox could soothe you into your dreams of voices and foxes.

Soft fox, little beast, stroke the face of my weepy son once more, whisper ethereal things, don't let him stay half-here.

# 82

"A-*eh*!"

From the capital of his borrowed crib, my son, the titan, lifts his little head.

I think I hear the creaking of pulleys, barely sustained by curiosity. Face-down, trembling with effort and equilibrium, he gazes out at the horizon of his bedroom, which is larger than the world.

# 83

You yearn to do before you can. More than a draft, you're an exaggeration of a human being.

Your waterless stroke and grounded wingbeat are more your own than any movement of tomorrow, when you'll believe you've mastered the mystery of your body.

The road you've traveled is nothing short of epic: you haven't moved a single inch, your eagerness intact.

# 84

"You haven't seen anything yet."

"Just wait till he starts talking!"

"And he's not even walking yet."

No. No. And no: you've taught me that you're already complete, just like this, drooling, diaper-clad, master of the moment. I refuse to define you by what you still supposedly lack.

If only all of us finished beings were capable of your economic marvels. One by one, you exploit your resources with an intensity you'll lose once you earn the rest. You're perfect in your shortages.

"He just woke up."

# 85

"Hey, baby!"

"What's his name?"

"How old is he?"

These mouthless entities have more to tell you than it seems. They want to take you in their arms, even though they only wave from a distance. They're full of arms and doors. They mean no harm. Don't touch them.

Those people are people. You know what I mean?

# 86

No one answers at my hotel-haven when I knock on the door. Our first hours in different cities have changed the rules of space: any farther than my arm is an abyss.

My back aches with the weight it lacks; I catch myself lifting air. I turn toward every wail or yelp I overhear, pouncing where you aren't.

I walk this place of silence—its corners of introspection—and your tiny face flashes up from the walls, in my eyelids, in any trinket glimpsed.

Not very many nights ago, I would have called this freedom.

# 87

The urgency of home shoves at my back. My steps quicken, the keychain protests in my pocket, a void throbs in my arms as someone grows faster than time itself.

The small guest in my home is its true owner. I belong to the doors he opens.

# 88

I lose sleep over the money that doesn't go far enough for you to have everything. No one can or should have everything.

In your transitory bliss, you still lack material whims: you only covet the festivities of being attended to, the luxury of now. I'm rich if we play.

Lurking at the end of the hall, money lies in wait for your slumber so it can strip me of mine.

# 89

I know, I know, its noises summon you, its design rings a bell, its images speak the tongue of the present.

We suspect you'll like it far too much, it'll become our favorite enemy, your memory's central frame: your veins are made of it.

We call it te-le-phone.

# 90

I wake in the middle of the accident, the choking fit, those slow plummets from balconies and staircases I reach just barely too late, following threads of fog. I'm the catastrophe father: instead of resting, I lose you when I sleep.

"A-*eh*, a-*eh*!"

Until you rescue me, rooted in reality, which sometimes hurts us less than dreams do.

# 91

When other hands touch you in the emergency room, and your folds become a secret to be studied, and we surrender you to a science that doesn't know your name, and you stare back at us with a half-voiced cry, suggesting a compassionate reproach.

Then I tumble desperately in love with the chance that's made you who you are, transforming me into this unprotected protector.

# 92

"Tee-tee-tee, tee-tee-tee."

The sound of rain on the roof will be a constant in the skies you cross. The sun behaves more like a theory of what we hope for, and which rarely comes.

There's nobility in rain. Not the romantic kind, but the eroding one: it scours the limits, offers a soothing sustenance.

"Boom!"

As I ruminate the drops, you've bitten a maraca, and the thunder's in your mouth.

# 93

The flavors of the world. The ones read by your mouth in its book of water. The one that sputters in a green apple, sharpens the glimmers of a lemon, softens the gums of a pear. The tomato's clean urgency, the honest potato, the painted taste of squash. The submission of chicken, which maybe you'll reject someday.

The flavors of the world. The ones to come. All those, if I open my attention wide enough, that you'll reveal to me.

# 94

Thirsty for summer's blood, your breath fills with ripe berries. You stare at me, lips wounded by your greed, cheeks smeared with evidence of your pulpy crime. You let out an exuberant, acidic shriek. Red laugh, red day.

My son is a round-trip vampire. He absorbs the very energy he radiates.

# 95

I immediately sit you on my lap to test the tiny multicolored piano you've just inherited, to see if you're tempted by the feel of the keys. But you have other plans: you overturn the instrument for a look at its back. Are you seeking out the underside of the notes, the silence they hide?

Now that I think about it, you do this with everything you come across. Phones, pillows, coasters. Slices of bread, sneakers, magnets.

"It's because of the books," your mother translates for me. "He just wants to read the back page of everything."

# 96

What is it you find so hypnotizing about fountains? Is it the fall, the rhythm, the clarity? Is it the continuity of its promise?

Holding each other, we identify springs across our liquid city.

And I flow through your eyes if the water blinks.

# 97

We celebrate your first rainbow by the largest fountain we can find. It takes shape around your pupils.

What can I tell you about this reality that can't be touched, the color of what vanishes?

Cling to the contours they show us: they're realer than the rest.

# 98

Forty years ago, in this same wave, I swam with my father.

We plunged down deep and rose up again, blurry-eyed, facing the horizon. I believed in his fleecy forearms. They protected me by reflecting his fear.

Now I'm the one who holds you facing the ocean, and the future watches over us, and my gray hairs are new.

## 99

The day my grandmother died on another continent, you rolled onto your back for the first time. I was searching for a shore where I could grieve, and suddenly you changed position like an hourglass.

Then you did something like looking at me, and you laughed as if nothing could ever hurt us.

# 100

Crawling laboriously at the foot of the curtains, you play hide-and-seek. Your head blends into the cloth's white gleam. You've left with the light. You're gone. My life is unchanged.

Then your vigilant eyes reemerge, your overwhelming laugh. The fabric hums a bit, the current breathes. Here you are. Returned from the light. My life will never be the same.

So I approach the curtain and step over to your side.

# AND A MINIMAL MONOLOGUE

Too much work to reach things. Why don't they come to me? What's everything doing over there, so not with me?

I stretch my arm and it's never enough. The stillness of the things I want, it makes me cry.

If they slip out of my mouth, if they drop from my hands, then don't play with my eyes.

They talk to me. They seem to think I understand what they say. And even though I don't, I do.

All the strange music from their mouths. It's like I've heard it before. Before what?

I want to have the mouth. I want to say the music.

Everything is full of eyes. They're all so fast. They come, they talk, they go. It's hard for me to answer, their mouths have other voices.

The faces I know are my faces. The arms I live in are my body.

I crawl backward to get back to where I can't remember. I advance in reverse. I push, and I'm here less.

"This way," says *mamama*.

"Here," says *dadada*.

And there I go, I'm coming, farther every time.

I don't want to go to places. I don't want to know where we're going. Action makes me dizzy, I'm bored by real toys. I want to stay right here.

All I want is a fountain with its fountain, my wind in the leaves, all this I can't name.

When I set down my feet on *dada*, and he holds me up but not much, and I feel a tickle in my legs, and we look at each other, I feel happier than happy.

I'm never sure which foot goes first, my ankles slip, my knees jolt. It's not comfortable. I like it.

And I feel like something's really about to happen.

# II

~

# SMALL SPEAKER

For Telmo and Erika, my teachers.

*Son of my son am I!*
*He remakes me!*
José Martí

*Speech isn't a basic function,*
*it's a form of stubbornness.*
Pola Gómez Codina

# 1

The hard part wasn't standing up, but finding yourself there, abruptly hoisted to your full height. Now vertigo guides your steps. Distance becomes anxiety.

"There you go."

"Very good."

"Wait, stop, stop!"

You'll be amazed by how often you fall. It'll hurt us both. You already get to your feet much better than I do.

# 2

"Careful, please."

You're tempted by edges, their risk, their deviation. The door ajar. That table. Rungs. The border of the bed. That's where you want to be, on the verge of—

"Careful!"

At your age, they say, we don't fear such things. Maybe your fear is transitive: you delegate it.

"Please!"

A blow is your way of testing the texture of the world, the accidents of its shapes.

"Ahh, so close!"

Edges entice you, I suppose, because they're like you. Your radical incline. Your jutting-out in the restless light.

# 3

You drag your left foot when you walk. I wonder if it's some side-effect of crawling, a transitional gesture, or your own rhythm.

You interweave your steps laboriously, setting one foot in front of the other toward the unknown.

You limp: we walk together.

# 4

And I watch you run, fall, and stand unsurprised, as if it were all part of your method. You stumble without ever glancing down: you have a horizon—an object, a light, a pigeon—that guides your pilgrimage. Blessed are those who can imitate you.

I think of all the times I hurt myself trying to move forward. Of when you'll know about them. Of your clean patience. And of how, despite it all, those memories live somewhere, folded into you.

# 5

Ever since you discovered your fragile equilibrium, you push any object that will conspire with you: a box, a chair, the garbage can. This third object has a superior charm, because it's light and stinky and recounts what we've done.

You come and go, back and forth, porting our trash. By the time you find a place for it, you'll have figured out family.

# 6

I can no longer write what I used to. You interrupted everything and started it over. I can't find my old reasons, my old grammar, because now you're the one babbling between the lines. Because now it's you who speaks in my arms.

I can no longer write the way I used to, but not a single word has been erased: everything I've ever said leads right here, feeding the language we were born to.

# A

Somewhere between dependency and addiction, I tend to mistake our simultaneous bodies. That's why I decided to write in the third person. That's how we raise a language.

How to move from an umbilical cord to a longer bridge, there and back? I wonder what kind of movement might recover the *I*, which will be there for him as well.

The door trembles a little.

# 7

How to describe your little voice? Any attempt means a brush with failure, stutter, or cliché. All three are also mine, and they release me. I want our conversation free of any emotional police.

Your voice is the voice of a bird that doesn't quite know what gurgling is. Of some indefinite instrument trying out its timbre. Of a bell at the window, of this very breeze.

It's the voice of your inner monologue, the one I had at your age, the voice we recover by listening. Two neighbors chit-chatting forty years apart.

# 8

With our sleep shattered, as your mother healed the night's interminable chest, I took you in my arms. I whispered the songs that always soothe you. They didn't work this time. You cried on, impervious to music, as if you couldn't even hear the solace. Sleepless at another frequency.

And so, on impulse, I started telling you things. I described the moon, the stars, the wind. A tree with birds and apples in it. A small landscape composed of familiar words.

You went still in my embrace, didn't even rest your head against me: a strange posture I'd never seen in you before. Language won out over fear. It filtered into your unconscious. And at last we loved each other as speakers, too.

# 9

You scream out of habit. You've become an onomatopoeia. When you open your mouth, the sounds follow a course, a possible meaning.

"When will he stop."

"Patience."

"I've run out."

Your silences are no longer a mystery, a state in themselves, but the anguished preface to speech, the rage of almost.

# B

The rage of his inability to tell us what he wants, or what he imagines he's telling us. This fury of open vowels. Sudden striker, he arches backward, resisting everything.

His age of elocutive urgency lies between a mouth crammed with intention and the words-in-progress. Not yet exactly a speaker, but no longer preverbal.

The sweetest, darkest part of him is vanishing. Contrary to my expectations, I realize I'm going to miss my wordless boy. And here I wait, impatiently, for his next self.

# 10

You consume your mother with your greed for life. Her breasts have gotten infected several times: she trades her health for a fever. Her immune system joins a dialogue of love.

She rarely complains. Which worries me, you know? Sometimes I imagine her shrinking so she can expand in you, as if you contained growing particles of your mother. Her calcium, your skeleton. Her muscles, your strength. Her fat, your thighs.

I pick you up again and feel our flesh made future, both of us aging slowly in your beauty. I hold your mother in my arms. You hold me in yours. Bit by bit, you sustain my corpse. I'm the posthumous baby you rock to sleep.

# 11

I fail to lull your nightmare. You now demand your mother, her panacea breasts. I feel suddenly rejected, foreign, as I did in my exile. And foolish for feeling this way. It's about you, not me, I know. But here I am, on the other side of your needs.

You teach me, by postponing me, a subtler art. And so I apprentice myself to my own limitations.

## 12

Your purée smile is over. No longer do you gnash light with your gums. Now you have the laughter of an involuntary beast: a mammal with a toothbrush. You flay. You crush. You hunt time.

"Ow."

"Hey!"

"No, love, no."

"I said that's enough!"

In the industrial jungle of your birth, those fangs will serve you little. But Mama and Papa are edible beings. And in the long run, I'm afraid, hard to digest.

# 13

A feather with teeth. As soon as you gain weight, some virus, bacteria, or mysterious cycle enters the scene. You wane for a while, retreat to where you started.

We've tried everything: eating together or separately, sitting you down in a highchair or in our laps, letting you improvise or marking a rhythm, with a fork or without, metal or plastic.

"A little more, juuust a little more."

"Your spoon."

"Like a big boy."

"One more. Please."

Your hands wander, ignoring the nutrition tables, the maddening percentage curves. And, all of a sudden, your body subtracts its conquered mass.

You're a person with a year and a half of life behind you: your mouth already masters the language of vicious cycles.

# 14

Teaching you to eat is a mirror. Face to face, we chew. Exchange hands in our mouths. Pupil to pupil: a pair of olives. I'm not sure who's following who. We're a system of attention, a bond of nourishment.

Occasionally you pause and point at objects whose names you've been digesting. It might be a piece of fruit or a glass, a pencil or a dish towel, a book or a tin can. Whatever you focus on, I deliver it to you.

And then you point at me.

# 15

You split the soft part, skewer precariously, lift your pulse to your mouth. You eat your danger.

I veer from vigilance to enchantment, pride to alarm. I shudder at the fork's strange angles.

Anxious, I seize my chance to scarf some leftovers. Your mother and I fast to watch you eat. A starving love.

# C

With every syllable shaped by his lips, he invokes the fragments of his world.

*Ma* is his mother and is more, and is the sea, and the apple, and everything that burns, and even a hovering fly.

*Pa* is me and is the light when it goes out, and is bread, and sweet potato, and the plastic pail, and is also the pigeon he chases.

*Ta* is ball, window, guitar, and, often breast.

His broad ten-syllable repertoire propagates his senses. We're both his translators and his disciples. His tongue-twisting language deserves a dictionary. My son, my neologism.

# 16

There's something I want to confess to you, something that frees me from this unofficial, vaguely hetero bashfulness I was always taught.

You're so beautiful, son, that it knocks me flat. I mean you're far too handsome. Look at your discrepant lips: the lower one cheerful, the upper one melancholy. Your flounced eyelashes. Tweaked nose. Cheeks that return the caress they're delivered. Can you explain how on earth I'm ever supposed to say *no*, set boundaries, put things in perspective, and other essential nonsense?

# 17

I watch you in your nakedness, radiant at your tiny scale. I blink and the image blurs.

I'm unfamiliar with these tears of pure admiration, confronted with the autonomy and shamelessness of your beauty. I feel like I haven't done a thing about it, aside from sheltering you on my shoulder, with all my doubts in tow.

Well, okay, maybe your feet are mine. You stumble toward me, confirming this.

# 18

I knead your feet like fresh bread in the making. I travel the destinations of your steps, feeling out every path that awaits you.

You ask me to blow on your right sole, drying the sweat of your adventures. Then the other one Your eyes grant me the measure of our devotion. You know how much it's worth: you've learned it much faster than I.

Beside us, a diaper, bloomed with shit, synthesizes the union of our bodies.

# 19

In the shower, your attention catches inexplicably: there, dangling in the air, surprising no one else in our household, is my strange thing, flanked by a pair of what-are-those whose function remains mysterious to you.

You like to point it out in all its evidence. It's just what you see.

I wonder if you find any resemblance, if you suspect it concerns you somehow; if you can even sense the secret seed of your origins. I'd give anything to know if you know.

## 20

You come over to watch me pee standing up. I explain what I'm doing with my body, narrating every gesture, and your attention tells me that you remember what awaits.

I wonder when you'll learn that your father actually sits down to pee, just like your mother, and has for many years. I've returned to my origins just so you can keep yourself clean in public restrooms. You study my raining member. We both focus on its pitter-patter.

I know genitalia doesn't necessarily define you or mark your fate. But this anthropological ceremony seems to engulf us in something transcendental. As soon as you press the button and the cascade roars, I resume my principles.

# D

In the vast divide between the monosyllabic and bisyllabic realms, there's room for two whole feet. My little one has transformed into a bipedal speaker.

Before, as if following a hermetic code, we had to guess which part he'd retain of every word, which scrap of sound he'd yank from it. Verbal communication, more deduction than dialogue, was rooted in polyvalent particles: *ma*, *pa*, *ta*, and so on, traversing infinite homonyms.

But now we've reached the revolution of two syllables. Their variants multiply in geometric progression, and misunderstandings begin to retreat. The world goes crisp and nuanced in his mouth, a lens focusing on what he says.

I can understand you, son. Now what?

# 21

"*Be? Be? Be?*"

You hear bells all the time, or you're always waiting to hear them again, in the church across the street, across the neighborhood, on every street you walk, a distant buzz, ding dong round the clock, we have to run outside to celebrate them, it unsettles you that we don't pay attention: they're there for a reason.

"*Be? Be? Be?*"

We'd better make it on time: a mute bell leaves you overly alone. Your prayers are by ear.

"*Be? Be? Be?*"

Our house has become a belltower, we have an entire playlist of churches from all over the world, bells addressing you in a single language, pealing against the roof of your mouth.

# E

His mother has noticed that as she weans him, little by little, he tends to mix up words he once clearly distinguished.

Now he's christened his ball *tatai*, and breast has become *tetai*. They're just a step away from being identical. To distance himself from his mother, to explore his own body beyond hers, he kicks a lactating noun.

For baby *pap*, which nourishes him without milk, he uses the same word as the one he uses for me: *papai*. He wants to mistake me for what he eats, needs to name me after his food.

Don't leave just yet, *bebei*. Remember what I taste like.

# 22

Inflamed with your liquids, emancipated organ, your diaper: I heft it in my hands. Now I'm fond of piss. I thought I hated the smell, until yours burst into my olfactory vocabulary.

When it opens, this Proustian garment yields memories of who I was before you. A whole lifetime without knowing you. And I didn't even miss you: it was happily squeamish, my self without you. Without everything that leaves your body. This piss of your creation. The kidneys that unite us.

And I wash my hands, almost regretful.

## 23

You're outraged when we dress you. How dare we. Who do we think we are, sheathing you in clothes whenever and however we like? Why not run around buck naked instead?

You writhe with vigor: every garment is a shackle.

It's one thing to clean your sweet little bottom—which we certainly do—and quite another to exploit the protocol.

Come on, Papa, you're not that dumb, I tell myself you tell me.

# 24

I was more your father today than on other mornings. I woke you without hurry. I removed your heavy diaper and put on a new one: you entrusted me with your dawning body. I dressed you singing songs that followed the rhythm of your legs. I made coffee for your mother (milk, no sugar) and shined her black work shoes. I felt perfectly in place, in this here and now that doesn't exist.

## 25

After half a history of practice, of knots and tumbles and gymnastics, you've learned (more or less) to undress yourself. You navigate your body.

You regard us proudly, showing your little chest, your minimal sternum. Meticulous ribs. Shoulder blades of implausible dimensions. Round, taut belly. Reddened member.

You clutch your diaper, folded into a ball. I try to take it away from you and you duly defend it. At your age, there are things you no longer tolerate. Everything inside it belongs to you.

## 26

The clothing of our household is your paramount mission. You extract it from the washing machine and bring us one small garment at a time, eager to join the community.

"Over here, love, here."

Sometimes you stumble, sometimes you get distracted. You're not always sure which direction to walk, or if you should deliver the clean clothes into my hands, or perhaps pick up what I've set aside and return it to the womb from whence it came.

# F

"You?" my son asks, pointing to his own small chest, when I offer to help him at the foot of the stairs.

He hears it all the time, so he's made it his own. He takes pronouns very seriously.

"You," my son confirms, answering himself.

He nods, looks up, and embarks alone. With every conquered stair, he rises closer to himself.

# 27

Your personality fills with nuance, with strokes fleshing out the sketch.

Now you know how to mimic a sincere smile. You use it when you want a wish to be fulfilled, or when you feel some adorable gesture is expected of you: you transform it into a grimace, a flash of what we might call proto-irony.

Tonight's smile was different. I held you in my arms at our bedroom mirror. In the shadows, your head against my shoulder, I crooned to you, thinking you were half-asleep. I closed my eyes to focus on the ebb and flow of care.

When I opened them again, I turned back to the mirror and found you wide awake, peering at my reflection, waiting for me to recognize you. Then you invented the delayed smile: the one from a past that copies our image.

# 28

Your new pastime is pretending to be scared. You look at yourself in the closet mirror and make faces, grazing yours against the one that confronts you. You open your mouth as wide as it can go. You bare your new teeth. And you howl, spooking the other boy in there.

Few adults can play at their own fear, startle themselves in the second person. I'd ask you to teach me, but I don't want to scare you by telling you why.

# 29

I have no choice but to swallow these pills to fall asleep, because we all have our gaps and blackouts, because light is a difficult activity. If there's one thing I detest, it's the ridiculous hero's cape, concealing a body that fails to say

"I can't, son."

"I'm going to disappoint you."

"Can you help me?"

"I'm scared."

When you emerge from the bathroom wrapped in a towel, like a creature plucked out of the sea, you embrace your mother—scent of cool breast, imminent sleep—and I dry your hair, just like every night, with this plastic thingy that reminds us of planes taking off.

Today I'd really appreciate it if we could curl up together, if you could grant some of your accidental protection. I think of all the things we silence in the half-tongue of love. I decide to approach your koala body, clinging to its maternal trunk, and—dryer in hand, flight in progress—I whisper into your ear.

And you open your arms to me, and we rock each other, and we recover from the worst things that befell us before birth.

# 30

Let the record show, perhaps for the purposes of future therapy, that the crown jewel of your lexicon isn't *mama* or *papa*. Nor is it *water*, *tree*, or *ball*. The first word that's truly thrilled you, the word you identify in an ecstatic trance and repeat every day, is *fan*.

That's right, my boy. Fan.

Impossible to see one without your arms starting to whirl. You seek them out, detect them, murmur to them, want them to purr in your path, command every slumbering fan to rise, their blades to rejoice, want every ceiling transformed to wind.

They don't run in the winter, which disappoints you. Yes, there's something missing in every word. Cooling expectations: what's that called again?

# 31

You're a consummate individual, a full citizen in the cruel summer of this planet.

Now you have a fan.

We bought it for you at a neighborhood appliance store. A man named Juan Manuel assisted us. As we crossed the doorway, you stood stunned, in a state of revolving shock, before the forest of fans.

Some tall, with wide round bases. Some rectangular, thrumming at ground-level. Others small and convex. Still others like caged turbines. All running, twinkling.

Except for one, cheaper, made of black plastic, unplugged in a corner.

Need I say which one you chose? Juan Manuel tried to dissuade us.

It vibrates, lucid, in your bedroom. You always want to play in its proximity, like a bodyguard. Your colorful balloons drift at its whim.

# 32

How to compare the patient act of building a tower with the chaotic thrill of causing its collapse?

We watch you—terrorist of play—raze projects of pedagogic colors and intentions, annulling would-be civilizations like an anarchist King Kong.

Or maybe it's the other way around, and the purpose of your demolitions is to begin anew. Forever focused on everything to be done.

# 33

Your legion of invisible animals keeps growing. Now we have a hen and some chicks, a turtle, a pair of frogs, a green cat, and a blue one. There are rumors of sheep and even a turkey. No news yet about the cows.

We invite them onto the balcony, taking care that their wings, feathers, tails, and paws don't get tangled. And we shut the door as quickly as possible, so that the mosquitos of reality don't devour your pale little legs. I'm sorry to confirm that you share your father's allergies.

We feed them breadcrumbs, corn, fruit, and seaweed. We're not quite sure what seaweed is; we look up some photos. You learn that frogs like insects. So you beg me to open the balcony and let all the mosquitos in, so the poor things can have their lunch.

# 34

When I was about your age, walking with my mother in the San Telmo neighborhood, we stopped at a toy store. Among countless options, I chose the toy I wasn't supposed to want.

I pleaded insistently. I wanted that one, that one. And she refused, confident that she was protecting me. There were so many nice, appropriate things! I'd requested a toy kitchen; my mother tried to save me from my mistake. Instead I got a ball, a sword, who knows.

Today your grandfather, with his snowy beard and widowed memory, has brought you a gift. Happy birthday, my dear: this kitchen is ours.

# G

Waving a finger in the open air, like the pinwheel in a flowerpot, he entertains himself by puffing out refusals.

"*Nu, nu, nu.*"

*No* is candy, and he loves it, relishing its sweet roundness. *Yes* is also *no*: he rejects whatever he'd originally asked for. He doesn't even want what he wants.

We're mired in a methodological dilemma. If I say no to his negations, will he nod to contradict me?

"*Nu, nu, nu.*"

Logic is a bad pacifier.

# 35

More than the date itself, what's exceptional about today is the way you register time. Never again, for the rest of my life, will you not know it's my birthday, nor what a birthday is.

You're still not inscribed on any calendar, its rituals of finitude. I see you at the edge, at hand's length, at no distance at all: you're intrigued by the songs and candles. Next year, everything will be different. We'll celebrate our births, their fleeting fortune. We'll start to be snuffed out together.

Now blow a little harder, please.

# 36

You frolic with his anticipatory ghost. There's a secret in this toy-stocked room: your father's father will vanish far sooner than you deserve.

Your grandfather waters the clocks when he plays with you and a soft ball, a plastic flute, yesterday's balloon.

I look at him and almost fear touching his hunched back. I approach slowly. His body is in mine.

# 37

Today we went to your grandfather's house to take care of my mother's violins. We took down the cases with care, opened them lock by lock (click! click!), and unveiled the wood.

We dampened the sponges, dryer than bricks. It's not the same water as the kind we drink, see?, it's de-ionized, but anyway, that doesn't matter. We returned them to their boxes. And lay them down beneath the masts.

I wasn't sure if you should be within reach. But in the end I let you pinch the loose strings. The room filled with avant-garde arpeggios. Memory sang out of tune.

That's the closest you'll ever get to playing with your grandmother.

# 38

Tirelessly you seek out the green watering can, although you can barely hold it. You wet the patio and balcony at all hours. You even water without water. Our guardian of dry plants.

Your most far-flung ancestors flow forth. A distant line of roots your incipient nose may catch a whiff of.

"Fill the can, please."

The voice that speaks doesn't sound like mine. It's my father's, or my father's father, consummate gardeners both.

"It's always full."

It doesn't really matter who replies.

# 39

Today, for the first time, you've told me a story from the past.

When you tripped by the bookcase, you caught your balance. You regarded the shelves that failed to graze you, pointed an accusatory finger, and rubbed your skull.

A few days back, in this very spot, you'd received a blow that made you cry and opened a rift in your succession of presents.

Now you have a memory: you know what hurts.

# H

"Car went."

That's what he says, no less.

*Car went*, preterite and all. Now he announces that there's something going; not everything is the present. Things leave.

"Car went."

We stand still, listening to the murmur until it's gone.

And there's someone who moves away, and it's my past son, at the speed of words.

# 40

"See things."

"Do you want to—"

"See things!"

You rub an eye with a dirty finger, begging for your favorite game: going out to read everything around you.

You come closer and ask me with great solemnity, full hope. The plan is observation. Discoveries will follow unprovoked. Because of seeing things. That's it. Full stop.

I never went so far.

# 41

They just flew over our heads. Staring steadily in the midday light, you command the sky to drip flocks, as if you were milking it.

"More. More birds."

If one passed and then another, why stop now? Does beauty grow tired?

"More? More birds?"

Such are your pleas: you look up and make a wish.

## 42

I've never needed so much money or come up so short each month. What exactly is left of consumption, when you grab, shake, celebrate everything without any sense of purchase? What possible or rebellious meanings do all these goods acquire, with their accumulation of shapes and textures, when you haven't yet tried to possess them?

I used to hate malls: you resignify them, running this way and that, dismantling our little sermons. Who cares what your professor mother or bearded father may have to say. Attention changes economics.

# 43

Here, my boy: take this envelope filled with time, of backaches and border bodies, of women birthing babies who resemble you, of lost jobs, mutual hatreds, blood, and doubts.

This envelope is filled with money and penury, of forgeries, of toys for some and bullets for others, limits and laws, riddled schools and hospital beds: it's filled with shit, just like your diapers.

This envelope contains a handful of rights, plus your oppressions. Your good, your lesser evil. All of this will be yours.

Yes, love, right there, in the ballot box. That plastic bin. Good luck to you.

# I

"Not that one. This one."

Decisive, he makes his choices. He delves into the binary structure of desire, its juxtapositions. We watch the path of his finger, which illuminates or suppresses at his whim.

"This one. Not the other one."

We obey with linguistic wonderment. We're the slaves who conceive the master and think they get to choose their condition.

## 44

"How are you?"

"Tired. How about you?"

"Tired too, yeah."

Your mother and I barely talk about anything anymore, except for you, which means there's a lot to talk about. Every once in a while we talk about how much we miss talking to each other.

"I miss you."

"Me too."

"Since when?"

"I'm not sure."

The logistical machine steamrolls its own operators. Here we remain, crushed by this intensity, unconditional as damage. If love and resistance engender each other, then we know where we come from.

You've taken all our space from us. You've opened a vast field before us. Both things are more than true.

And I hold your hand and we walk at a beginner's pace, and I owe your mother every step.

# 45

An arm bumps me in the dark. I open my eyes for the umpteenth time.

"Is that you or him?"

The bed, once ours, has been invaded, or repopulated by your minimal body, and I wonder when it will be reasonable to redistribute our spaces. And who, in the end, will be left more deeply alone.

Your mother nurses you in a state as liminal as our mattress: she's neither asleep nor entirely awake. She reads your movements in the shadows, exhausted.

"That's your own arm."

# 46

We have lunch alone, in a pleasant place, for the second or third time since you were born. Our fault, of course. As a couple, we were always so independent that now we don't know how to manage our dependencies. Our story had a center of its own. No one prepared us for your radiance.

Your mother has bought herself a pair of beautiful yellow boots. She exudes levity, like in the old days. I regret that I'm not wearing new clothes, although I've carefully chosen my outfit.

We raise our glasses. Clumsy, we smile.

I shouldn't talk about you, not right now, but I can't help it. I confess and we look at each other with relief. Our glasses clink. And we sip our theme.

# 47

You have dinner with your grandfather at home so we can go out. If everything goes smoothly, he'll put you to bed, with a papal bull to skip your bath.

Liberated, we graze.

The messages that reach us from base camp are reassuring. You ate well. Poop: no problem. You fell asleep right away. Beside you, your grandfather beholds you with pride.

We even order—can you believe it?—dessert.

Back at home, everything is silent and shadowed. All we can hear in the background are the tireless blades of your fan. We make our way, trying to float on tiptoe. We whisper. It's a simple hypothesis:

"They're both asleep."

When we enter your bedroom, what we see is this: seated in your little chair, bolt upright, you watch your grandfather snoring among the toys and cushions. Sleeping like a baby.

# J

Some days ago, he stopped repeating only nouns, as if listing his treasures, and the verbs that name his impulses. Now he holds the key to other senses. He's found the secret particle. A bridge between semantic archipelagos.

He's discovered a preposition.

Astride the back of his *at*, my son goes wherever he wants. With *at* he tells us *with* and *in* and *for*: the open vowel of company, setting, and motivation. He uses it constantly, grasping its scope.

With a pair of trifling, crucial letters, the lever of language, he'll build his world.

# K

We translate him bit by bit. He grows apace with his grammar, and with our mechanisms for deciphering it. We live on the edge of understanding each other.

"*Mo a om.*"

We stop the stroller on our way to school. He looks at us, convinced he knows what he's saying. Puzzled that we don't grasp the obvious. His mother frowns in concentration.

"*Mo a om.*"

It's not that he doesn't know the words: we're the ones who are ignorant of his lexicon. His eloquence is here, right in front of us; the precision of every syllable, the melodic curve.

I focus as hard as if I were scrutinizing a text in Latin. The options shift and rustle, straining to assemble themselves.

"*Mo a om!*"

Suddenly, everything becomes clear. Telmo. At. Home. He wants home. To stay home. He doesn't want to go to school. Finally, finally.

And now that the author's intention has been properly translated, we keep pushing his stroller against his wishes.

# 48

Today, at school, you rearranged your sadness. Instead of mourning your captivity, you cried while pointing at all your other crying classmates.

When someone went to comfort the child in question, you'd cheerfully return to your toys.

You spent the whole morning this way, all over the room, rehearsing pain in the pain of others.

# 49

I'm running late to pick you up from school. As I hurry, I picture you in a corner, near the window, your body touched by the light, attentive to the door's activity. I wonder if you have any sense of abandonment, if our closeness has immunized you somehow, if this is a matter of my own childhood.

From our very first memories, parents have shown up late to school, late to parks, to parties, to appointments with the pediatrician. Parents show up late to the intimate secrets that involve them most. Late to their children's bodies, to the very shock that they exist. Late. Parents. We're late to everything, except to death.

When I burst into the classroom, hair unruly, hiding my distress as best I can, a couple of your pals are still there and you seem relaxed. I try to suspend myself in our hug, compensate for who knows what. But you're far more interested in showing me a limping zebra and your drawing of a blurry sun.

# 50

In your social life away from home, you tolerate the purées you've always hated, wake your friend from his nap, and have been initiated into a kind of dance in which crocodiles are pets.

You've lost purity, because you let the world into you. You're better out there, broader, odder. You're educated in chords. You sound strange. You're you.

# L

He loves naming zero, one, eight. The moon, the stars, the airplanes. Orange, yellow, blue. Lemon, apple, avocado, which is called *palta* on the other shores of his Spanish-speaking heritage, a difference he's familiar with. Geraniums, roses, cypresses. Monkeys, pigeons, and especially crocodiles.

Everything has colors, sounds, or flavors that are interconnected somehow. His science and his menu are a synesthesia.

Of the ship, he likes the anchor. Of the slide, the stairs. Of our flowers, the pot of earth. Is he seeking metonyms for roots?

## 51

I'm a terrible dancer. Or so I've thought since childhood. Did I mistake clumsiness for shyness? All this time evading dance and other eyes. A whole lifetime following an inner rhythm.

Until you showed up and respooled my legs.

Now we dance together every day—I hope you'll remember—in a kind of tribal celebration without a cause, an antidote against some hostile future.

And at your school people even think I love it.

# 52

Your first guitar doesn't fit in your arms. I've just brought it home for you to demolish with gusto. The days of its pegs are numbered; your curiosity will survive its strings. But I couldn't resist: you're always strumming your belly.

I present it to you with great ceremony. You accept the guitar with a firm grip. Then you turn it over and rap the drum.

# 53

The Argentine music we put on for you brings me to tears. Its childlike cadence darkens between the lines and reseeds my ear.

You—you who are Spanish without knowing it, you who have sounds, fruits, and pronouns I discovered in my transplanted childhood here, you who absorb songs and have every shore ahead of you—would you dance with me?

# M

It will take him months, weeks, days to discover that his father was born in a faraway land, learned a different verbal music. I'll become a brand-new foreigner again, on the brink of babbling.

Surrounded by incipient vocabulary, our conversations fork.

"Let's put on your sweater, which they call jumper here."

"Would you like some French fries, which are called chips here?"

"Look at that big truck, love! It's called a lorry here."

For now, he fluidly accepts our duplications. I wonder what he'll do when the tribe and its customs begin to impose their hierarchies. Will he feel like he has one hemisphere too many? Or the other way around: will migratory magnetism do its work? Will he someday heed its call?

Meanwhile, we study geography.

"Where do I come from, son?"

"From home. Home."

# 54

Ever since you've started recognizing antonyms, your eyes seek opposites. What hemisphere does each object belong to? You're concerned about *empty* and *full*.

Full: the drawer with clothes, the shelf with books, this glass with water. Empty: the fruit bowl, your shoe on the floor, the glass in your hands. Full, your table laid with paint of all colors. Empty, every page, awaiting your drawings.

This week you're trying out intermediate concepts. They're so counterintuitive! You accepted *medium* with a look of resignation. Something neither large nor small, deep down, is absurd.

But your body appreciates *warm*, and you calibrate the water with restless fingers. In the laboratory of your plastic tub, I try to suggest that we don't always want extremes. For a moment, you look convinced.

"I want very warm. Very!"

# 55

When I travel, we act out the truth. We seek ceremonies that will take the shape of memory.

We pull out my suitcase together. You push it flat and we open it. You help me fold my clothes, or, better put, you help me wrinkle them. We review the names of the different garments: nouns filling a vessel. You love tugging at elastic, tossing socks that bounce and roll away.

We carefully zip the suitcase shut. You feel strongly about checking the mechanism over and over. The taxi awaits. You push my luggage on its wheels. Then I seize the moment to rehash the details of our goodbye. The forms of transportation, the places, the number of days on my fingers. I wept at what you said the last time.

"Big plane. Small papa."

I'd never heard exile and distance so neatly summarized.

If you're not home when I come back, your mother and I join forces to stage reality: a few minutes before you enter the apartment, I go back out, luggage in tow. I wait until you're inside, then execute my reentry.

The heart is nothing but these narratives that slowly give it form.

# 56

I ask you to draw the flag of the countries I'm visiting. A way for us to cohabit, share some ground. You like Latin American flags, or maybe you've just noticed how I celebrate them.

Argentina's flag has an air of the sun in childhood drawings, a house in the distance. In your view, the Bolivian flag is much prettier than the Spanish one, because it also has green in it. And green, as everyone knows, is important.

Today you sent me the flag of Ecuador: a solar-yellow strip, a vigorous blue smudge, and some red scratches that convey the accidental beauty of haste. Looking at it, it's like I'm more fully here now, I've landed in the homeland of shared thinking.

Your flags are the opposite of patriotism: they seem surprised to symbolize anything, they approach their fellows with wonder. We're trying to separate them by continent. You don't find it easy, much less logical. You're puzzled about the Mexico/Italy situation: they're all the same colors. Aren't they?

# 57

I'm about to take off, bound for an island, and the blades of my aerial terror start to whir. I don't like this tin can one bit. As it rises—not very smoothly—my feet tingle, my shoulders brush my ears.

Between the two of us, no matter how emphatically they call it a *helicopter*, it's just an enormous *fan*.

The sun blinks. The sea looks like a threadbare rug. Its creases can't be ironed, just like our clothes at home. Remember the sea? We saw it one afternoon. You wore a little hat that bothered you.

It's ridiculous how easily I can picture you as an orphan. And yet speaking to you protects me. We're so close that I remember you even after death.

It's not vertigo: it's a child.

# 58

When I call, you demand I appear.

"I see? I see? I see?"

We activate the camera. As soon as I smile, you swipe your bear paws at the screen. My image is your prey. I can't tell if it's excitement, curiosity, or rage.

Your hand seeks your father's face, trying to connect with it in a single stroke. As if, by making brutal contact, a presence could return. Your mother holds you up to me, encouraging you to accept a more elliptical love.

"Don't touch, sweetie, or he'll go away."

Fulfilling her prediction, the call cuts out again. Your father goes dark. I reappear at once. And you try again. As quickly as you learn, you refuse to understand how it works.

I hope it'll take you much longer. You're teaching me not to give the body up for lost.

# 59

When I travel, you ask your mother to reproduce (that's exactly the verb: again and again) videos of moments we spent together. Us, playing and running and dancing and eating apples. Instants that don't expire, that are always there, available, identical, on a timeline your consciousness organizes in enigmatic ways.

To what extent are these images a representation? In the novel of your emotions, do you absorb them as substitutes or presences in themselves?

I'm on the phone, hence I'm not there. My presences and absences are contained in a single device. Very much like a family.

# 60

The landscape overwhelms you, distracting us from our scribbles. Too much reality. You clamber up the seat of the train.

"Not with your shoes, son, they're dirty."

The trees are pretty, yes, the stripes of grass, the mountains. The animals are very nice, the houses, all that stuff. But you're not in the mood for it. And you know just what to do. Peering through your digital lids, you repeat, impatient,

"Off, off, off!"

But the windows aren't working.

# 61

This is floating. The Archimedes principle, let's call it. It means entrusting your body to the water, just as we volunteered our embrace to strangers when we were babies. Arms wide open: imagine you encompass an entire shore, knowing many others await you.

That's right, very good. Just like that.

Head lifted, always alert. If you want to submerge it, so your ideas can swim too, then take in all the air your nose can find, raise your hands skyward, and blow, blow hard as you descend.

Will anyone protect you? Of course they will. Of course they won't.

# N

Lately, the word *broken* causes him hyper-semantic distress. As soon as we say it, tears spring to his eyes, as if he could sense that nothing is totally reparable.

"Don't you worry. Papa and Mama will fix it."

And in his look of half-hope, of initiation into harm, I see something beyond repair.

# Ñ

As soon as our son began to speak broken language, he also began, occasionally, to hit his mother. They're light, timorous slaps, as if he were exploring a sacred law. We censure his act. He regrets it. And reoffends.

Before words, his vocabulary lacked for nothing. He felt complete that way. But now that he knows he barely knows how to speak, I sense his discomfort with his limitations. He has to fight to express himself. He hears the echo of his omissions.

The nameless violence of the mother tongue.

# 62

I classify risks by size. I do the same with your possible aggressors. Hierarchies of age, masculine intimidations. I had an ugly childhood, son. I don't want to project, but I do. And these kids reigning from the heights of the slide only reinforce my fears. They're slow-developing beasts and victims. I know exactly what they're doing; I saw their future when I was small. I had an ugly childhood. I don't want to project, but they shove you, they threaten you as you ascend the rungs. I separate their arms from your body, we look at each other, and we're an octopus in motion, a single being in different times.

# 63

They're too strong, their bodies equipped with springs you haven't yet found in yours. They play with scary speed, graze you like airplanes, take impossible leaps, scale iron bars in defiance of instinct or logic.

I get it, I get it. We've all played in this park.

Now that you know, love, drift a few meters from this vulnerable father who watches you and climb, very slowly, onto the little red horse.

# 64

It's the first time you've slid down the slide by yourself. You did it in your own, wholly recognizable way.

You shrank back at the top, both hesitating and gathering momentum. You let yourself fall at the speed of pleasure without harm, regulating the brakes of your sandals. Your velocity slacked. You landed almost at a halt, master of your limits.

And you got to your feet, euphoric, applauding your debut in the adventure, running right back to the stairs—which are no longer quite so tall for you, no longer quite so close to me.

## 65

I already wince at the blows you'll meet along the way. Who knows how time-resistant the fiber of your sweetness will turn out to be. It'll last, I suppose, though stained with violence here and there.

It's not that you're an angel: you're just experiencing a benevolent version of your fellow creatures. Does this certainty belong to me or the street? If I get ahead of myself, will I protect or poison you?

"Maybe it won't happen to him."

"It's better if we know."

"It depends on the school."

"And on whether he does martial arts."

You give the other kid your ball, a red leather one, somewhat deflated; gently, he gives it back.

# 66

You run through the hedges. You revel in their angles, the traps of all geometry.

Growing up—would you agree?—means getting lost on purpose, pursuing your problem as you play. And you shout

"Good! Very good!"

With your hands held high, smiling triumphantly, when at last you spy the exit that will let you reenter the labyrinth.

# O

We play at inventing silly languages. We exchange phonetic nonsense. He's much better at it than I am, maybe because he has so few references. His favorite non-word is something like

"*Kiapa cublú.*"

I struggle to undo my lexicon, betrayed as I am by the traces of roots and homophonies. Sometimes I succeed if I omit the vowels and emit instead a cascade of consonants. Inaugural chatterbox, he says

"Very good."

# P

A different hypothesis: with this made-up speech, he's testing a different framework. Breaking the hierarchy of interlocutors.

In his mother tongue, our son feels that he has a disadvantage. He often doesn't know, can't get where he's going, or is misunderstood. He grapples with every phrase. He's a disciple. By contrast, improvising languages is a horizontal game. There, in the absence of meaning, he's sovereign of senses.

When I listen to the whims of his mouth, it feels absurd to speak in any exhausted grammatical code. I try, little by little, to forget my tools, my ground. A forty-something child.

# 67

When I leave the house with an air of adult-on-a-mission, I wonder if you find my activities mysterious. What kind of life could be out there, without you? What is Papa up to on the street, which is so wide? What important affairs demand him?

There's no mystery at all, my son, and little importance: don't ever overestimate my absences. Wandering out and about, I fulfill my duty like a husk. I'm thinking of you almost all the time.

And now, if you don't mind, I'll need my coat, my keys, this impossible grown-up face.

# 68

"Don't cry, it's just for a day or two."

It nourishes you that your mother works. I'm not talking about the cost of the menu you devour, but the family characters your memory cooks up.

"I'll be back as soon as you know it, I promise."

You'd rather have a unanimous mother, but these parentheses are part of her speech: every time she leaves, she keeps teaching you from afar.

And when, finally, she steps out into the city without your weight, her body is cleaved with a helplessness we never admit to, so that our contradictions won't bring us to our knees.

# 69

It's good to feel you heavy in my arms. I notice, son, how your pounds mean time, how the present fattens when I lull you to sleep, or when I carry you on my back to the limits of my modest strength, or when we look up at the stars on the balcony.

"How many are there?"

In my prior life, I never felt the summons of the species. No unfulfilled mandates. None of that. I was as happy as permitted by good taste. What I couldn't have imagined was your weight: this mutual matter that sediments here, between being and ending.

I never missed you or pleaded for your name. You simply arrived at the border of light, installed a meaning there, and remade me. It's good to feel you heavy in my arms.

# 70

This, my hernia, is yours. I offer it to you like a little parcel of guts.

"The operation was straightforward. Three small incisions."

Walking together brings a secret pain, joy, and tear. At least I've put a little of my body into it. A tiny fraction of what your mother gave for you to be here.

"Four to six weeks. Then back to normal life."

What's normal life in our chaos, this beginner's love, my not knowing what to do?

"You'll be fine. No question."

And meanwhile you, minuscule and gargantuan, extending your arms.

"No heavy lifting for a while."

Come into my arms, break me and heal me.

# 71

There seems to be a slow self-portrait in your jigsaw puzzles. You need to put them together several times a day, as if to make sure that they're still available, their meaning hasn't vanished.

You've got the one made of wooden cubes, which yields horses, mermaids, and castles. The one with the numbers, too, and your eternal dilemma between nine and six. The one that groups things together with their geometric shapes: are cakes seriously pentagons? The one with monkeys napping in the shade of a tree, which is most welcome as you get ready for bed. And there's the vegetable puzzle, too, which you complete during meals.

You started with two or three fragments, a vocabulary of sorts. These puzzles are increasingly large and complex, scale maps of your reality.

Maybe you suspect this is another piece.

# Q

Play is a form of obsession. His favorite obsession, this ABC puzzle. He undoes and remakes it, affixing notions with a discipline I've rarely seen. He lives in a state of research. I try to learn how everything is learned. I knew once, then forgot.

He organizes letters without the arbitrariness of alphabetical order. He's interested in the lines that can be associated and distinguished. An O isn't the same as a Q. The E isn't an F. The P skims the R. The N: a Z on its feet.

It suddenly seems so odd and capricious, the sketching of these signs. The more I observe our son spelling things out, the less I understand how I know what little I know. In the presence of his hands, I'm illiterate again.

# R

The world is alphabet soup to him now. He throws himself into the composition of neighboring symbols, insists on deciphering their hieroglyphics. When he finally succeeds, he seems to wonder, then what? Or is that the whole point—an end in itself?

In a moment of distraction on my part, he takes my phone into his room. I watch him pause in a corner and start to type, making the face of all-important tasks, his tongue peeking out.

FFZS8 RÈCH

I A5KI LB N Z 1FN ZZ

That's his message. It convinces me.

## 72

You inspect the books on our shelves: you want to verify that the white parts really don't say anything about anything.

"Nothing here."

You repeat it with a sense of skepticism, as if you already knew there's no such thing as empty discourse. You pass the ant-trail of your fingertip over every floating space.

"Nothing here?"

It's more a question than a statement. You doubt what you say. Just like each of these pages.

# 73

If I toss my little ball of crumpled paper into the basket, you grant me a tepid nod. But if it falls far from its target, you're all cackles, pleas for more and more.

You've discovered the pleasure of mistakes. I watch you making wayward shots, parodying expectation: instead of seeking my approval, you celebrate your failures aloud.

Hoops of the wrong color.

Letters in mismatched holes.

Unsustainable towers.

This jigsaw puzzle where nothing fits.

After all the effort to absorb the rules, blunders are our new luxury. You can't even imagine the gift you're giving us.

# 74

We didn't have much fun today. In response to nearly everything, including your favorite games,

"No, I don't want to!"

You hit me on the leg and testicles with uncommon marksmanship, yanked on my beard without hesitation. You refused to get on the carousel I ran over to, sweating. And all you cheered for was an apple.

"Not green, red, red!"

There were no memorable observations. No anecdote shook me to my core. Maybe these tenderly mediocre days are what makes us who we are, what keeps us close forever.

# 75

To hone your drowsiness, we go out into the night and look up. We review the trappings of the sky, trace their tethers with our fingertips. We name the stars, errant planes, and, if we're lucky, the moon.

You locate it much faster than any adult eye. You light up as soon as you detect it, like in a theater. Your lunar instinct feels to me like a kind of omniscience. An omniscience from your stroller.

Your rapture at the sight of it, conspiring up above, inducts you into a cult of vagabonds, dogs, poets, and owls. Guess how many of these categories your father belongs to?

# 76

The story about the owl who falls out of his nest, gets lost, and goes looking for his mother—I don't like it. It omits the father from the get-go, takes for granted that he can't be there.

You request it every single night, as part of the order that sustains your hours: the tale of the creature who only aspires to return to his cultural nest. I read it to you, somewhat listlessly, for the umpteenth time.

"Time to go to sleep now."

"With Papa?"

# 77

What kind of intimacy is this, more naked than flesh? We watch you thrash at the edge of the bed, a tiny broken bellows. I touch your burning skull. We cough in unison: it's the orchestra of the shared body.

We collect viruses and bacteria, furnished with the stubborn shield we call love. Gastroenteritis, fevers, rashes. Conjunctivitis, blisters, bug bites. And, of course, your pervasive mucus.

"Any Kleenex left?"

"No."

"Paper towel?"

"Nope."

Our family is a laboratory for every possible contagion. Of course, this includes the unconscious. And there's no cure for that, as you'll find out.

# S

Unable to sleep, he didn't ask me for water tonight. Today, for the very first time, he wants *more* water. A vast distinction. What a different kind of thirst, the one with an adverb tucked under its tongue.

"More water. More. More water."

I'm soaked by the drops of grammar his wishes absorb. More than before is a lot, maybe everything: it's the awareness of an expectation.

"More, kiddo?"

"No. More."

# 78

You don't distinguish between *here* and *there*. You don't need those coordinates for your penguin-walk. As is true for all of us, your grammar is your view of the world.

You ask me to sit down beside you on every bench or step. I obey. We look ahead. We stay for just a few moments in this position. Then you leap up again and the cycle starts over. More than taking a break, you seem to be seeking the sensation of taming the present, taking possession of microscopic time.

"There, there."

You say it as you point, finger stained with who knows what, at the space you already occupy.

# T

He's discovered the adverbial forces: he slips them into every sentence he can muster.

"Ball? Park? *Now*?"

The only moment he dominates is called, indeed, *like that*. It has the frenetic rhythm of satisfaction; it lasts only as long. Later, when we can, we'll talk about *later*.

If something was ever in any place, he hopes it remains *there*. Everything remembered deserves permanence. *Still* is a more emphatic *now*, charged with a will he recognizes: may things stay, not go.

Papa. There. Still.

# 79

Your teacher informs us that you danced with Emma, whose smile is much like yours, both shy and sassy. When Emma hugs you, you stand completely still, overwhelmed by a semantic field you haven't yet explored. You like being with her, but not when she gets too close; you like company in individuality, each playing their own game.

We receive reports from school about how you eat, if you've slept, how much you poop. They summarize your body in a grid. Which inspires my gratitude and a pinch of jealousy: these used to be family secrets.

Your teachers frequent a side of you I don't know. They spend each day with another child, a character of yours we haven't quite discovered.

# 80

You sleep, we're told, hand-in-hand with your buddy Óliver, with whom you play a lot, and who hits you a little, and whom you hit a little. You hold hands for your midday nap. You breathe beside him, surrendered, in diapers.

If only the rest of us could return to the unnamed love between those two small bodies, with their imaginations still bare, prior to the wire fence of identity, without guardians of this or that, when sleep and wakefulness converge.

# 81

Your school has asked us, on the back-side of a sheet of cardboard painted with watercolor, for a few lines of poetry about wind. We moms and dads get more homework than any student.

I'll admit that I like this assignment, though: it feels tribal and necessary somehow. We've been repeating it since the air has blown, since words have migrated. Virginal, I approach my charge: I've never written a poem for children before. Except, of course, for the immanent child whose voice leads us.

As you eat an egg and some olives, I scribble on a napkin—the ancestral style of the twentieth century—my first semi-rhymes for you. I hope you like them, or at least that you'll be merciful.

*The air is in a hurry*
*to find its way back home*
*and thinks it's really funny*
*although it can't say why.*

*It makes a pleasant sound*
*as it shakes all the leaves:*
*hey wind, make me a house*
*like where the birdies live!*

*It messes up our hair,*
*then huffs and puffs and blows.*
*I hope it won't erase*
*my smile that peeks right through!*

# U

It's no longer a question of linked nouns, occasional sensory adjectives, compass-needle adverbs. This, ladies and gentlemen of the Royal Academy of Wonder, is an entirely different matter: now he's got syntax.

The net that measures the sea. The cast of his puzzles. The board that lodges every piece. His days of babbling are over: in his speech, there's no baby to be found.

Isn't it a marvel? All of hell is left for the telling.

# 82

You spent some time chasing after the exact name for everything. And, as a few vaguely Germanic idealists would also do, for essence everywhere.

"What is that called?"

"What *is* this?"

You'd admit no imprecisions, no ambiguous replies. If we tried to call a spade a rake, you'd protest, incredulous.

"Naaah!"

"Not that, that not."

Now the game of language has led you to the second square. You no longer care about the original truth; you care about the meanings you can build with. You ask me to turn on the fan.

"You mean our helicopter."

And you nod, satisfied. Then you ask after your mother.

"She went out to play the violin with a seal."

And you request further information. To keep going, to tell you more.

It's called fiction, son. The part the truth is missing. I have a feeling that you're going to like it.

# 83

Your mother opens the door. She whistles, barks, and meows. Pajama-clad, you summon your invisible animals to join you for breakfast.

We make room for the bodiless dog, the silent cat, and, of course, your crocodile. We take care with the tail, which is long and spiky. An expert navigator of such hazards, you roll it up with a wave of your hand.

As you eat your oatmeal and lemon yogurt, your mother goes to your room and returns with a plush crocodile, hidden behind her back. I try to distract you. She sets it—ah!—right on top of the table.

"Look at that, kiddo. It appeared!"

You pick up the toy and examine it intently. You shake your head, disdainful.

"Not that one. The real one."

And you push it away, leaving room for the invisible. Then you lick the lid of your yogurt.

# 84

I unfold your stroller at the school entrance. You lift your head and focus on a white bulb, round and smooth.

"That, moon."

I hesitate for a moment. You know it too well for it to confuse you now, don't you?

"Well, yes. Metaphor."

You nod in agreement with who knows who. And off you go, hopping along, ready to play elsewhere with the world.

# V

We can see a castle from our balcony. Magnetic. Unthinkable. He spies on it every night before bed. We point at its towers. We admire it from afar, because it's a castle.

Today I suggest we visit it and he shrieks with exhilaration. *Go? We can?* You can do almost anything if you're a child. We put on our shoes, step out onto the street, head up the hill, and climb steps larger than his infancy.

And finally, right in front of us, radically strange, is the vision so often glimpsed.

"Castle! There! Castle!"

We rush to invade its spectral space. But nothing happens as planned: uneasy, he wanders around inside, glancing everywhere, as if he lacked something essential.

"We go? Castle? We go?"

"We're here, son."

"We go? We go?"

"It's here, you're right here."

"Castle? Other one? We go?"

At once I understand his tragedy: when he's inside the castle, he can't see it. His desire demands perspective. To be in a place means to lose it.

More than the impossibility of entering a castle, perhaps the worst thing is accessing it unimpeded. I hope my son never writes me the kind of letters that Kafka's father deserved.

# 85

You parade your energy through a sea of plastic balls and inflatable castles. Climbing has become a vocation. Leaping in your cadence.

Today, our adventures ended late: we're the very last explorers. I put on your sandals, and suddenly we behold the prodigious collapse of your kingdom.

The castle starts losing air. Its trembling edges stagger. They shrink. Helplessly, the towers melt until only their ruins remain: a multicolored fish.

You can't take your eyes from it: you're stunned that such a mass can be so precarious. Its ground seemed solid enough to trust. You believed in heights; they were merely this. Your body was there, and now there's nothing.

"Don't worry, tomorrow it'll get blown up again."

"I don't think so, Papa."

How can I contradict you?

# 86

"Sss. Ssso..."

That's what we're playing at: the great invention of the rudiment, the only language in which more than two men in the same place tend to understand each other.

The object of your desire tangles between urgent feet. The path opens as it rolls. Your entire body seized with euphoria, you release your air and try to say what's happening:

"Ssso. Sssocc...!"

# 87

In your former vocabulary, its name was *tata*: this sphere inflated with anthropology. I hide it just in case; you always find it.

"Park, Papa. Park."

Who would have thought? Me, whose football-infused childhood I fled from, who always imagined a daughter practicing other sports, who swore I'd never impose the game of all games onto you, who never even dared hope you'd like it as much as I did—now I run and pant and beg you to stop for just a moment, please, loving each other behind a red ball.

# W

In my arms, in his green pajamas, he approaches the window. He regards the other part of the house and points to his bedroom wall.

"We live there."

He states this with veteran certainty, like someone discussing neighbors he knows all too well.

"We *live* there."

The rhythm of his sentence stirs me. He could have simply said, emphasizing the adverb,

"We live *there*."

But he's stressed the verb instead: we live. Such confirmations are always welcome.

Then he looks up to the sky, counts two or three birds, and asks if there's any jam left.

# 88

You run to the couch where your mother spends a moment recovering from being a mother. You climb into her lap. Lifting her clothes, you formulate the command you've successfully disguised as a question.

"Milk?"

"After your bath."

"Milk? Now?"

"When we're getting ready for bed."

You paw her breasts, gauging her likelihood to obey, considering whether you can demand that someone yield their body to you. She shakes her head no. On the verge of defeat, your hands withdraw.

But suddenly a phrase leaps to your aid: the same one we're so fond of repeating. You assume an expression of moral gravity.

"Mama. We have to share!"
And a cheerful nipple gleams in the dark.

# 89

You no longer wail as you did in distant, recent times. You've discovered something more effective: instead of tantrums, dialectics. On wounded legs, in blue sandals, comes this monster of logic and love.

You accepted the rule that you must give me your hand in sight of any car. But today we walked down a steep hill together, easy ground for tripping.

"Give me your hand, love."

"I don't want to."

"Your hand, son."

You raised your head. Looked at me calmly. Pointed didactically ahead of us.

"Papa, no cars. See?"

And thus, invoking the father, you managed to disobey me. The moon seemed to applaud.

# X

Listening to him speak, I sense that the great question doesn't start as philosophy, not even as logical fumble. At first it's just structure, a linguistic reflex.

"Why are you crying?"

"Why."

"Do you know why water falls from the sky?"

"Why."

This small mimesis has morphed into statements that gradually forge a formal habit, an archetype of reflection.

"I don't know why."

He intersperses this phrase in unexpected contexts, almost arbitrarily.

"Good tomato. Blue sandal. I don't know why!"

*Why* involves the eloquence of the world when it's new. It means the urge to look. It doesn't ask for an answer, just open ground.

# 90

"What was your favorite part of today?"

Your question moves and grieves me. Shouldn't we always ask this before the light goes out? When did I stop?

To buy some time, I ask about yours. After all, you're the inventor of this game.

"My favorite part was eating apple with Mama."

And you look at me, eager for my reply, convinced it exists.

And you were right.

My favorite part of the day, the one that rounds it off, the one that saves it, was when you asked me the question I can't let myself forget.

# 91

"Goodbye, tree."

"Goodbye, fountain."

"Goodbye, chair."

You don't only bid farewell to people and animals. You repeat the ritual with every object you've paid a bit of your attention. Because you breathe life into things by engaging with them, or because you sense they all live some life more or less quietly.

First you concentrate; this is very important. You look steadily before you leave it. And you wave a hand like a bouquet of time.

"Goodbye, black doggy."

"Goodbye, balloon."

"Goodbye, Papa, goodbye."

# Y

"I decided not to."

That's what he said when we insisted he brush his teeth today, too. Sitting up in bed, legs spread wide, eyes bigger than himself.

"I decided not to."

I find it difficult to resist such conclusive syntax. He could have said what he always does:

"I don't want to."

But tonight there's a language party. He's thought about it, he claims, and has decided not to: it's a highly meditated conclusion. His mother fights back laughter.

With his tiny blue toothbrush in one hand and his tutti-frutti toothpaste in the other, I wonder what to do now. How to react in a way that prevents cavities without dismissing his Socratic adventure.

Intrigued by the plot that he himself has set in motion, our son studies us, suspecting that a different story is about to begin.

# 92

You devour images from a prehistoric era of your own story. I wonder what part of the brain you stimulate with these past-present exercises.

"Pictures, Papa."

"Which would you like to see?"

"Papa and me."

What will you remember of our four-handed childhood? All these experiences that were once impossible to affix in the memory? Or the mp4 videos, detached from their referents, that saturate my phone?

## 93

"This is my mother. See? My mama. Delia. Her name is *De-lia*. She has very long hair. Black. Yes. She has a big, big smile. She loves violins and coffee. And the ocean. Like you, of course. No, she doesn't love soccer as much. She does things at night. She eats late. She's always in the mood for ice cream. Okay, but dinner first, okay? Big, big smile. Sometimes she blows out smoke. *De-lia*. She's from far away. No, she can't come. Meet your grandmother. She taught me how to talk."

# 94

"It's weird."

You think, my boy, that everything is:

"Weird!"

And you repeat it incessantly. This is your manifesto, an aesthetic school with a single tenet. Everything is very weird, precisely because we look at it.

How weird, that cat in the window, the empty fountain in the sun, the bell clanging, your toy sleeping, our half-inflated ball. How weird, those trees, their restless limbs, the wind calling out to them, every fallen leaf, the damp earth, that passing ant.

It's weird, son, isn't it? Both of us here, in time, sharing matter, mixing our shadows together, our bones, provisional skin, unimportant blood, sacred chance, intuition, everything invisible, truly very weird.

# Z

Once he was an amphibian: he understood words but wasn't made of them. He got by, when the need arose, in his maternal speech, as we'd do in a foreign language. His body was his own authentic grammar.

But now he thinks and eats and runs and thrills and cries and sleeps with lexicon. Not a single non-verbal pore is left. There's no turning back: he's a speaker. Now the real game begins.

# 95

The first two stories he's made up, chewing on an orange in a park, go like this.

Once upon a time, there was a ship and it was sad because it had no water. It wandered around, all sad and lonely: it missed its water. Then there was a boy who brought some. He brought it from the sea. In a bucket. And Mama. Until the ship had water again. And sailed away.

In the second story, my son was sitting in a park, chewing on an orange, happy as a clam. And suddenly, emerging from behind a palm tree, he himself appeared. Right there, right in front of him. When he was a baby. Too small. He recognized him. And it wasn't him anymore.

**ANDRÉS NEUMAN** (1977) was born in Buenos Aires, where he spent his childhood. The son of Argentine émigré musicians, he grew up and lives in Granada, Spain. He has taught Latin American literature at the University of Granada, was selected as one of *Granta*'s "Best of Young Spanish-Language Novelists," and was included on the first *Bogotá-39* list. His novel *Traveler of the Century* (FSG) won the Alfaguara Prize and the National Critics Prize, was shortlisted for the International Dublin Literary Award, and received a Special Commendation from the jury of the Independent Foreign Fiction Prize. His novel *Talking to Ourselves* (FSG) was longlisted for the 2015 Best Translated Book Award, and shortlisted for the 2015 Oxford-Weidenfeld Translation Prize. His collection of short stories *The Things We Don't Do* (Open Letter) won the 2016 Firecracker Award for fiction, given by the Community of Literary Magazines and Presses with the American Booksellers Association. His most recent titles translated into English are the novels *Fracture* (FSG), *Bariloche* (Open Letter), and *Once Upon Argentina* (Open Letter); his selected poems *Love Training* (Deep Vellum); and the praise of noncanonical bodies *Sensitive Anatomy* (Open Letter). His books have been translated into twenty-five languages.

**ROBIN MYERS** is a poet and translator. A 2023 National Endowment for the Arts Translation Fellow, she was shortlisted for the 2024 Queen Sofía Spanish Institute Translation Prize. Recent translations include *We Are Green and Trembling* by Gabriela Cabezón Cámara; *Death Takes Me* by Cristina Rivera Garza (co-translated with Sarah Booker); *Bariloche* and *Love Training* by Andrés Neuman; and *In Vitro* by Isabel Zapata, among many other works of poetry and prose.